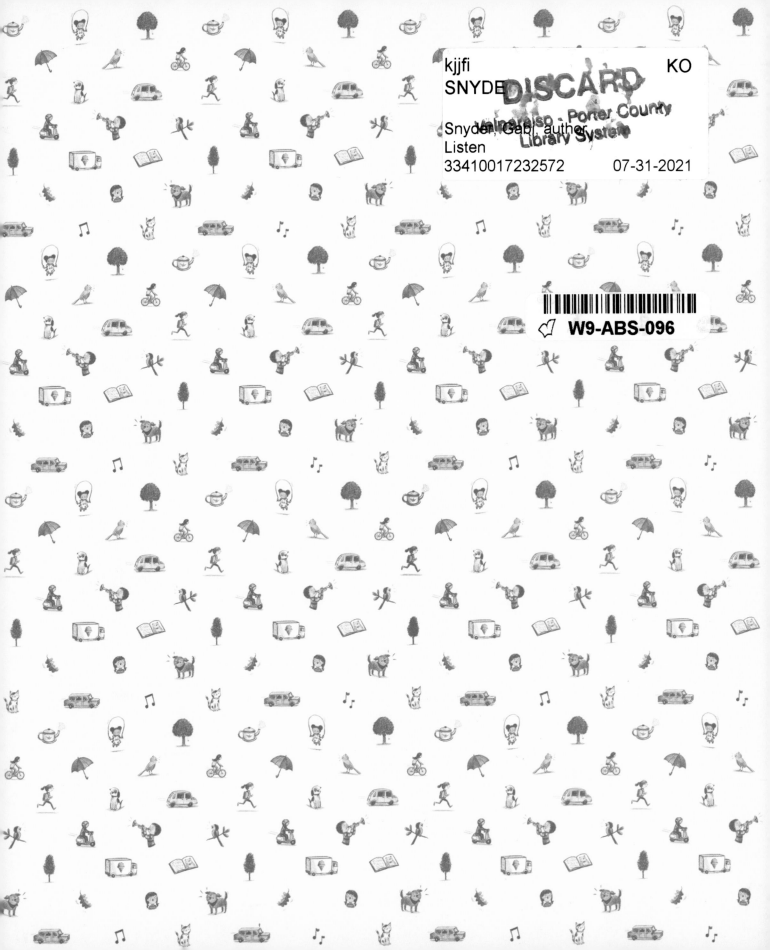

To my dad, who showed me how to listen in nature.
And to my mom, who showed me how to listen with empathy.
—G. S.

For Olivia and Sophia
—S. G.

SIMON & SCHUSTER BOOKS FOR YOUNG READERS
An imprint of Simon & Schuster Children's Publishing Division
1230 Avenue of the Americas, New York, New York 10020
Text © 2021 by Gabi Snyder
Illustrations © 2021 by Stephanie Graegin
Book design by Chloë Foglia © 2021 by Simon & Schuster, Inc.
SIMON & SCHUSTER BOOKS FOR YOUNG READERS and related marks are trademarks of Simon & Schuster, Inc.
For information about special discounts for bulk purchases, please contact
Simon & Schuster Special Sales at 1-866-506-1949 or business@simonandschuster.com.
The Simon & Schuster Speakers Bureau can bring authors to your live event.
For more information or to book an event, contact the Simon & Schuster Speakers Bureau
at 1-866-248-3049 or visit our website at www.simonspeakers.com.
The text for this book was set in Scotch.
The illustrations for this book were rendered in Adobe Fresco,
Adobe Photoshop, pencil, and watercolor.
Manufactured in China
0421 SCP
First Edition
2 4 6 8 10 9 7 5 3 1
Library of Congress Cataloging-in-Publication Data
Names: Snyder, Gabi, author. | Graegin, Stephanie, illustrator.
Title: Listen / written by Gabi Snyder ; illustrated by Stephanie Graegin.
Description: First edition. | New York : Simon & Schuster Books for Young Readers, [2021] | Audience: Ages 4-8. | Audience: Grades 2-3. |
Summary: Illustrations and easy-to-read text urge the reader to go beyond the noise of the city to listen to a crow's
caw, rain dripping onto a sidewalk, and whispered goodnights. Includes notes about listening.
Identifiers: LCCN 2020045572 (print) | LCCN 2020045573 (ebook) | ISBN 9781534461895 (hardcover) | ISBN 9781534461901 (ebook)
Subjects: CYAC: Listening—Fiction. | City and town life—Fiction.
Classification: LCC PZ7.1.S65746 Lis 2021 (print) | LCC PZ7.1.S65746 (ebook) | DDC [E]—dc23
LC record available at https://lccn.loc.gov/2020045572
LC ebook record available at https://lccn.loc.gov/2020045573

LISTEN

Written by Gabi Snyder

Illustrated by Stephanie Graegin

A Paula Wiseman Book
Simon & Schuster Books for Young Readers
NEW YORK LONDON TORONTO SYDNEY NEW DELHI

When you step out into the big, wild world,
sometimes all you hear is . . .

But what if you stop, close your eyes, and LISTEN?
Can you hear each sound?

WOOF!

BEEP!

Do you hear a dog yip-yip-yapping from
window to yard to passing car . . .
or a crow cawing from wire to wire?
Listen.

Through an open window,
a teakettle whistles.
Listen.
Can you hear the slap-slap-slap of shoes
against pavement?
Listen.

Kids jump rope, thump-thump-thump.
Can you hear "hello" called across the playground?
Listen.

Listen past the crunch of gravel and the scrape of chalk.

Can you hear new words? Listen to each sound.
Some pop, like *quick* and *snappy*, while others stretch, like
looong and *leisurely*.
Listen.

Hear words of joy . . .

and words that sting.

Do you hear what your friend says?
Listen.

Can you hear what she's feeling, too?
A sob, a sigh, or even silence.
Listen.

Listen past the **NOISE**. . . .
What can you hear?

Rain falling on your umbrella?

brush-rush-hush

Wind through trees. Listen.

Can you hear the quiet?

Listen past the quiet. . . .
What can you hear?

Rumble of belly.
Whoosh of breath.
Can you hear the voice inside you?

Listen . . .
to nighttime **hush** and **whispers**.

Good night...

good night...

good night....

When all you hear in this big, wild world is
NOISE . . . stop. Close your eyes. And *listen*
to everything waiting to be heard.

MORE ABOUT LISTENING

Your sense of hearing: When you wake up to an alarm or voice calling, that's your sense of hearing doing its job. Your sense of hearing has evolved to work all the time, even when you're asleep. Have you ever dreamt of a barking dog or a ringing phone—only to wake up and discover the noise is real?

Listening: Listening is more than simply hearing. To listen, you must focus on one sound. That can be hard when there are many other competing sounds. But listening is important. We can learn a lot about the world around us by listening.

Attention: Hearing is automatic. You don't even have to try. But listening is a skill that takes practice. The key difference between hearing and listening is attention.

Startle response: Different types of attention use different parts of our brains. When a sudden loud noise—like a car horn or school bell—makes you jump, that's the simplest type of attention. It's called the startle response.

Bottom-up response: When a sound—like your name called across a room—draws your attention, that's called a bottom-up response.

Top-down response: When you give your full attention to something, that's called a top-down response. Like a radio set to just one station, your brain "tunes out" other sounds to allow you to focus your attention. It's easier to learn when your attention is focused.

Listening to feelings: When you try to listen to the feelings carried in voices, you may be able to tell when someone is sad or angry or scared. Listening shows caring and can make you a better friend.